Ramblings

P. Dinakara Rao

Virgin
Leaf
Books

First published in India 2014 by Virgin Leaf Books
An imprint of Leadstart Publishing Pvt Ltd
1 Level, Trade Centre
Bandra Kurla Complex
Bandra (East) Mumbai 400 051 India
Telephone: +91-22-40700804
Fax: +91-22-40700800
Email: info@leadstartcorp.com
www.leadstartcorp.com

Sales Office:
Unit No.25/26, Building No.A/1,
Near Wadala RTO,
Wadala (East), Mumbai – 400037 India
Phone: +91 22 24046887

US Office:
Axis Corp, 7845 E Oakbrook Circle
Madison, WI 53717 USA

Copyright © P.Dinakara Rao

ISBN 978-93-84226-49-7

Book Editor: Ms Kiron S Abraham
Design Editor: Mishta Roy
Layout: Chandravadan R. Shiroorkar

Typeset in Book Antiqua
Printed at Repro India Ltd, Mumbai

Price — India: Rs 95; Elsewhere: US $4

Dedication

This book is dedicated to my wonderful wife, Pramila Devi, without whose constant companionship I would not have been the person I am today.

About the Author

Now the Director of Spyn Financial Services Pvt. Ltd., P.Dinakara Rao started his career as a probationary officer in State Bank of Hyderabad. Trained in the field of Behavioural science by ISISD, with a Post Graduate Degree in Applied Economics, his speciality was in Personnel, Human Resource Development, Training and Corporate Credit. His skills gave him the opportunity to work in state banks across the country, on deputations from the State Bank of Hyderabad. He retired as Chief General Manager in the year 2005. After retirement, he worked as the Director of The Alpha Foundation and as Senior Advisor to The Maxwealth Trust associates of ICFAI, Hyderabad.

The author is happily married to his childhood sweetheart, Pramila Devi, and is the proud father of two wonderful daughters, Mrs. Sirisha Srikanth and Mrs. Shilpa Sharma. He has also been blessed with three lovely granddaughters - Akanksha, Ananya and Shivani. He wrote his first poem in 2006, titled *Buddhahood*, after which he continued to write poetry, culminating in the publication of this book, *The Ramblings*, by Leadstart Publishers. His other hobbies include photography, music (mainly tabla) and martial arts.

FOREWORD
By

Shri K.R.Venugopal

I have known my friend, P. Dinakara Rao, for three decades and my first impression upon meeting him then, and my view of him now, is that he is a perfect gentleman and a great human being. Cardinal Newman defined a gentleman as one who troubles his neighbour least, and I have known no better living illustration than Dinakara Rao, who exemplifies this.

Poetry has been known ever since human kind learnt to articulate emotions and thoughts. In its long history, in relatively modern terms, William Wordsworth defined poetry as "spontaneous overflow of powerful feelings" and "emotion recollected in tranquillity". The brilliant Matthew Arnold, known for his prose more than as a poet, spoke of poetry as "criticism of life". Arnold also attributed "high seriousness" as a necessary quality to great poetry. These are the touchstones any critic should apply while reading a book of poems.

In some form or another, we are all in search of the truth. One of the ways we do it is to try to understand it from the lives of people. In doing so, we also learn that a person cannot be separated from the way he has lived. Therefore, when I refer to emotions, tranquillity and high seriousness, I have seen these in the life of the poet that Dinakara Rao has been. I also know that "emotion" is often used by the unthinking as an attribute different from intellect, to downgrade the quality of the former. That is sheer illiteracy because an elementary knowledge of brain science will tell us how hollow an understanding that is.

Dinakara Rao is an embodiment of the understanding that comes from all these concepts, as will become evident when we read his delightful poems that showcase the truth as he experienced it, with the high seriousness he always brought to bear in understanding it. It would be very prosaic of me to list out the truths that he brings out in his work but the core philosophy of the poet needs to be mentioned.

The foremost among them is his very need for self-expression. That is the essential quality of any creative artist. That character of the poet repeatedly emerges through the poems in the 'Quest' section. The poet says that he has to summon his muse for his very sanity! That is how powerful his urge is, to write on the vital subjects that made his life distinguished. We love to read those because they are universal values as well.

What are they?

First and foremost of these is love as the core value of life. Its highest form is expressed in the poems under 'Young Love' and 'Companionship'.

The second - the love of, and unshakable faith in, God - comes out sensitively in the poems under the section on 'God'.

Third is the immortality of the soul. Its intimations come to us in the poems under the section on 'Old Age and Death'.

Fourth, the poet's impatience with the unfeeling rich and his concern for the lesser children of God is seen in the section on 'Suffering'.

And fifth, nature and the environment, and their protection, are espoused throughout the anthology, especially in the section aptly titled 'Creation and Nature'.

What distinguishes the effort of Dinakara Rao is his capacity not only to draw lessons from his own experiences but of others as well, for some of the experiences we see in his poems cannot have been personal to him. Such capacity for extrapolation is the hallmark of a catholic mind.

I congratulate Pasupuleti Dinakara Rao on this volume of poems and invite the reader to enjoy the outpourings of his imagination anchored in life, for a perspective that is different from the conventional.

K.R. VENUGOPAL IAS (RETD)
FORMER SECRETARY TO THE PRIME MINISTER
HYDERABAD

CONTENTS

WRITING FROM THE HEART – AN INTRODUCTION

Why can't people write poetry without a rhyme?
Undoubtedly, writing without a rhyme is not a crime
That poems must always be rhythmical is but theoretical
But literary critics undoubtedly will continue to be critical
That is why I write this poem, so simple and plain
Without giving these critics a chance to complain

GOD

God:Photograph taken by Author in Munich Germany

God like Sun which melts wax and hardens clay
expands great souls and contracts bad hearts
(Antoine de Rivarol -1753-1801)

EXISTENCE

I know not the real face of God Almighty
But most worship Him in the form of some or the other deity
Whether He is really there or not is irrelevant
As the belief that He exists is mostly prevalent
It is one's own faith that allows one to feel His presence
But for the atheist the whole concept is nothing but nonsense

FREE WILL

The myriad colours of nature serve
As paint in the hands of Creator
Some are dark, some are light
Some are bright, some are dull
On the easel of destiny
There lies the plain paper of life
The brush in one hand
The Creator lovingly moves
To paint a million patterns
Some are easy to understand and appreciate
Some are mysterious, beyond comprehension
Utterly unfathomable
Are our lives nothing more
Than his patterns to follow?
Is there really free will
To help us choose which lives to live?

FEEL

The shining water droplet, falling from a leaf;
The tiny ray of the sun, breaking through a dark cloud;
The microscopic bud of a bloom opening up;
The smell of fresh earth, after a light drizzle;
The humming of a honey bee, gathering sweet nectar;
The flapping of a small bird, as it learns to fly;
Feel His presence; He is everywhere.
In the toothless smile of an old beggar,
In the falling tear of a wailing baby,
In the faltering step of an old man,
In the rosary beads of a praying priest,
In the faithless arguments of an atheist,
Feel his presence; He is everywhere.

THE ALMIGHTY

The ever-nagging doubt gnaws at my belief
That HE is there to protect me, which is a great relief
The heart full of feelings latches on to the Almighty
Though the world presents gods of such variety
And all the religious heads cause such a cacophony
Creating a cauldron of conflicting ideas without symphony
Oh, Almighty! When will you finally choose to come down,
To clear our minds and save us from such a meltdown?

SEARCH

The wandering spirit
Searching a higher plane for guidance
The searing doubts about His existence
Dulling the soul's radiance
Logic, reason, rationale
Masking the instinctive, inner intuition
The scarred spirit
Begging for the healing touch of the divine
Will my search in my own world be futile,
Despite being guided by my wealth's might?
Oh, lord above, show me a sign
Guide me with the beacon of your kindly light

GOD

HE
From whom
Everything emerges
Finally only He judges
Whether we lived life purely
Or committed those unforgivable sins repeatedly
The path to heaven is undoubtedly narrow
But the golden path will lead to sorrow
Be wise, repent, seek the forgiveness of the Lord
He is the one leading you to your heavenly abode

DIVINE PRESENCE

Surrounded by the cacophony of the modern world
The mind wanders into mystic meadows
The retreat, the solitude, the stillness
The mind merges with the heart and hears
The sound of silence
The rustle of leaves
The rush of running water
Drags along small pebbles
In its mobile embrace
By divine grace, how blessed we are
In your eternal presence

LIGHT and JOY

He is a deity for some and sustenance for many
He exists to bring light and joy to all
He is full of magnetic power but never compels anyone
They all revolve around him but he stands alone
No one can touch him or hug him but everyone can feel him
I salute the selfless one, who is source of energy to all

Creation and Nature

*The weary sun had made golden arc And by the bright track
of his fiery car Gives token of a goodly day tomorrow
(william Shakespeare 1564-1616)*

CREATION

The wild and the subdued
The beautiful and the barbaric
The magnificent and the insignificant
The aggressive and the submissive
The lofty and the lowly
Oh, Nature! What an example
Of unparalleled Creation you are!

THE WIND

A gentle, cool wind caresses the cheeks of a smiling child
The light breeze ruffles the wavy curls of a rustic girl
The strongly scented winds carry secret messages
And loving whispers of a lover to his faraway love
The stormy winds toss the ships in the sea
And shake and shudder the planes in the sky
Cyclonic winds blow away cars, dwellings
Uproot mighty trees and cause mountain slides
Winds without discrimination touch
And affect the lives of all living beings
Oh, gentle and mighty winds!
Be the messenger of The Almighty and bless us
Forgive us but do not curse us

SANDSTORM

Shifting sands reflecting the setting sun's golden hues
Waiting for the weary camels to tread on its diamond-dusted path
The sandstorm covers the oasis with a golden blanket
The waving palm tree's branches wear a thin veil of dust
The unwary traveller gets caught in the stormy sand
Seeking shelter behind his camel to protect against golden arrows

DARK CLOUD

The thirsty forest clamouring
For the drops of nectar from heaven
The hidden flame waits for a chance
To ignite the whole dry grassland

The little breezy angels heaving
And pushing the heavy dark cloud
To meet the majestic mountain top
And evanesce into a billion shiny pieces

Teary downpour, like blessings
Answered by the gods of heaven
Come to quench the parched throat
And dull the flame of the hungry forest

THE RAIN

The pip-plop of lovely rain drops
Falling and dancing like happy little elves
Touching the grass and turning into drops of dew
Merging with the creeks and making them gurgle
Kissed by sunlight, refracting a million colours
With gay abandon they fall on everyone
Black, brown, white or yellow, as they are
The showers of God's abundant love

DROPS OF WATER

Scattering millions of tiny pearly drops everywhere
Falling on rooftops, rafters and on rusty nails
As if they were God's most blessed gems
With no discrimination and with joyful glee
 Like naughty children eager for their mother›s embrace
Splashing down on Mother Earth with gay abandon
Causing little muddy puddles for children to play in
Or merge into the mighty oceanic father
These life-giving and life-sustaining watery droplets

FALLING LEAF

The gentle wind blowing
The slender branch waving
The browning leaves quivering
Like a flock of birds shivering
With their colours changing
And their stems weakening
The leaf falls floating
Like a lost soul wandering
Can it blame the wind
For its eventual fall
To the earthy ground?

WINTER

The snowflakes fall
Like the white feathers of a fallen angel
The white blanket covering
Mother Earth, to keep her cool
The shrubs and bushes burying
Deep into the earth for survival
The tree branches decked in pearly snow
Languidly moving like pregnant women
The bird perching on the snowy branch
Waiting for the call of its coming mate
The children with snow balls in their hands
Engaged in mock battles for victory
The homeless shivering and cursing
Fate for their miserable plight
The teenage lovers trying to feel
The warmth of the body through heavy woollens
The winter, is it a curse or a blessing?
It all depends but it is undoubtedly
A cold present from the warm heart of The Almighty

WHERE ARE YOU?

Are you the droplet that falls from the mountain peak?

Are you the fire in the volcanoes, deep inside the earth?

Are you the dust particle in the centre of a raging tornado?

Or the foam on the tip of the highest wave of a tsunami?

Or the ray of the burning sun, in the hot, arid desert of the Sahara?

Or a faded green leaf, falling in the Amazon forest?

Or the sound of the gurgling water, from the springs of the Himalayas?

Or the wailing of a hungry child in the village of Ethiopia?

Or the wrinkle of an abandoned, destitute mother in Nigeria?

Or the stick in the hand of a blind old man of South East Asia?

Reveal yourself to me, oh secret, hidden, Creator of all!

NATURE

The whisper of cool breezy winds

The thrum of waving branches

The rustle of falling dry leaves

The chirps of gathered birds

The gurgling of creek's water

Pause, listen and open yourself

To be one with nature

AS THE SUN SETS

The rays of the setting sun break through the dark cloud
Reflecting silvery light on the still waters of the pond
The croaking frog welcomes the warmth of the last ray
The falling twig causes a ripple in the pond
The insect on the leaf battles against buffeting wind
A world of sounds turns mute as the sun sets
Imps and elves ready to jump out into the moonlight
To make merry along with the angel of night as she walks in

THE BEGINNING

The emergence of the unknown
Into the vast eternal universe
The seed once sown
In the womb of the would-be mother
The pangs of growing
And the slow awakening of the conscious
The first rays of light
Pouring into soft, hidden places
The cry of the emerging
Echoing and shattering the surrounding silence
The unscripted story
Yet to be told
But so many hands grabbing
To write their stories
On the empty slate
Of an unfolding life

ALWAYS REMEMBER

The slow-falling drops of rain
The ever-dripping mountain dew
The roll of pebbles in the flowing creek
The soft sounds of a toddler's steps
The never-ending chatter of teens so young
The shy smile of the blushing bride
The glowing look on the handsome groom
The stooped shoulders of the shuffling old
The warts and wrinkles of beauty that aged
The serenity of those departed from their earthly cage

MOTHER EARTH

Mother of all, always abundant and ever-giving
Impartial to the core, selflessly caring for all flora and fauna
The insignificant insect, the mighty Elephant
The roaring Lion and the flitting Butterfly
All are equal before her loving eyes
Suffering silently the savages committed by humans
The plunder, the pillage, the deep and indiscriminate digging
For ore, for oil, the mad and meaningless destruction
Of forests, the pollution of rivers, lakes and oceans
She offers prayers, to put some sense into man
For their own sake to be more merciful
And come out of their tiny windowless cocoons of ego and greediness
To be a part of a vast, beautiful and bountiful universe

LIFE

The fallen raindrops dancing on golden leaves
Like water fairies floating down with the sparkling rain
With the flapping of their tiny golden wings, the wind stirs
Causing the forest leaves to shower down
While the rays of the setting sun spread golden hues that soothe
I would like the life I choose to be just as beautifully simple

Young Love

'Tis better to have loved and lost
Than never to have loved at all
(Alfred Lord Tennyson 1809-92)

CUPID STRIKES

Burning cheeks, quivering lips, eyes misty
Emotions in turmoil and tangled up quickly
Steps falter, words stuttered, affecting sobriety
Distant footsteps and the rustle of a dress
Feelings are too intense, I am a mess
What can I do, what shall I do? Oh! Venus
Goddess of love, why have you allowed
Cupid to strike me with his flowery arrow?

TO BE MINE

Shall I ride on the mystical, moving clouds
To bring back the nectar from the heavenly spring?
Shall I take the seven strands from the rainbow
To make strings for my violin?
Shall I take the salty waves from the oceans seven
To make them dance on the golden beaches of heaven?
Please tell me, my dear, my brilliant sunshine
What shall I do to make you eternally mine?

WHAT SHALL I DO?

Shall I pluck the stars from yonder blue sky
To make a necklace of them for you to wear?
Shall I go into the depths of the turbulent ocean
To get you that pearl which is rare?
Shall I climb to the top of the tallest mountain
To get the elixir from the life-giving fountain?
Shall I walk on the hot, burning desert sands
Or swim to far-flung, isolated islands?
Tell me, my dear, what should I do?
To see your beautiful smile
And win a place in your pretty heart

DREAM GIRL

My feelings for you I do not know how to express
The weight of the whole world cannot suppress
You are the princess who rules over the kingdom of my heart
All the romantic poetry in the world to describe you would fall
short
Day and night my thoughts always around you hover
Oh my love, please tell me when this prolonged agony will be over

RIVER OF LOVE

My love for you is like a river
Seasons may change but it won't ever
Other suitors for your hand may be clever
But I will ensure that they fail forever
I will bathe you in a flowery shower
And make everyone else run for cover
With a soulful sword as my passionate armour
I stand at your doorstep as a vigilant guard
Protection against all the evils of the world

NEVER

There is magic and excitement in the air
Everything looks rosy and wonderful
The wind is cool, breezy and scented
The moon is golden, bright and shiny
The nightingale sings honey-dipped songs
There is a bounce in my step and lightness in my heart
I feel like dancing all night without a stop
As she said that she would never leave me

FOREVER

We walk together on the moonlit path
Stealthily escaping from our elders' wrath
The shining moonlight reflecting in your eyes
Makes my heart melt like ice
Walking hand-in-hand, whispering sweet nothings
We almost float in air with our heavy breathing
The sound of dried twigs breaking
Makes my heart start rapidly beating
I pray to the Goddess of love
To ensure our safety on this perilous journey
The happiness when we are together
Will be in my mind forever

DARLING

Oh darling, the love I have for you is formidable
The depth of my passion is undoubtedly veritable
Every moment I spend in your presence is delectable
I do agree, the problems we face are insurmountable
The opposition against our love is utterly detestable
But I do know that the union of our souls is inevitable

TOUCH MY SOUL

The wind whispers sweet nothings
The birds sing duets in dulcet tones
The heart flutters like a leaf in the breeze
The steps falter and the eyes become misty
The world spins as I spin, stops as I stop
The arrow of Cupid struck so deep
Oh, my love, touch my soul, touch my heart
As I will die without your magical touch

MIND AND MOODS

The extreme mood swings cause unwanted trouble
They rise from the depths of a mind's chaotic rubble
From ecstasy and joy, to agony and pain
The thoughts and feelings pour out like a torrential rain
How do I come out of this unfathomable muddle?
It appears to be a long and unending struggle

TEARDROPS

I will wade through the sea of your teardrops
To beg for your forgiveness without any props
No doubt I am the reason for your getting hurt
Of my abominable behaviour at being a flirt
Give me a second chance, my eternal flame
I swear that I will not make you feel the same shame

IS IT TRUE?

As I dance around with a smile on my face
He looks at me from the corner of his eye
Lightning strikes, it's as if I am hit with a mace
My heart skips a beat and melts like ice
Is he really the prince charming of my dreams?
Or the eternal Don Juan pretending to be my Romeo?
Reason says he is an illusion, with a loud scream
As I am the one with a leg affected by polio

FOR AN ETERNITY

My dear, why under such lovely moonlight
Pick unwanted quarrels and fights?
Is it not time to forget these petty things,
And whisper to each sweet nothings?
Life is short, time is fleeting, nothing is permanent
Let us bring our hearts closer and with love cement
We fly and soar and bathe in a moonlit shower
Our names etched on the clouds forever

ICE MAIDEN

Love for you was like sunshine
On the beautiful flower that is my heart
Love for you was like a mountain spring
To quench my thirst of deep desire

The crescent moon was like a swing
For us to sit and share sweet nothings
You were an oasis in the desert of my life
And I was a palm tree by your side

What happened suddenly to your love?
Why have you turned into an ice maiden?
Cold, calculating and utterly uncaring
A You have shut me out of your loving environ?

Quest

Quest:Photograph taken by Author at Kapell Brucke- Lucerne in Switzerland

He who knows others is wise. He who knows himself is enlightened
(Lao Tsze 604-531 BC)

INNER BEAUTY

Wise men tell us to look for inner beauty
But that idea gets lost when I look at a girl that's pretty
Coming face-to-face with an ugly one definitely makes me blink
But looking at a pretty one I know instinctively to wink
Is there any instrument through which I can gauge
Inner beauty, so that I can come out of this mental haze?
Is it really possible for me to love a face that's ghastly?
I do not think I can answer that in any way simply

UNFAITHFUL LOVER

The sparkle in her eyes turned into pieces
Of shattered glass reflecting the images
Of the unfaithful lover, ripping savagely
Through this fragile memory of mine
I can never go back to the way things had been before
I found about my lover's unfaithfulness
The sweet kisses turning into burning hot lava
The soul crying with the pain of mistaken emotions
The eternal doubt whether real love exists
Creeping back into my conscious, while the misery
Takes me down to the depths of dark despair

MIRROR

The broken mirror reflects faces
Distorted, crooked, beautiful, handsome
The inner turmoil shading the face
Being reflected in those million pieces
Which one is the real me, I do not know
Ugly, handsome, crooked or good
The totality of me is never shown
Only the different shades of my face
Put forth by me but may not be
The me that I want to be, so can I ever be the real me
When the face I show the world
Is the face the world wants to see?

WHO AM I?

Am I the savage from the jungles of the Savannah
Or a saint of the ephemeral world
Am I a sentry of the perilous underworld
Or a savant of the sophisticated gentry
Am I the embodiment of all human virtue
Or the quintessence of its innumerable wiles
Am I the confluence of conflicting emotions
Or the core tranquillity of the meditative world
I've searched like a wandering monk
Travelling to the far corners of the world
When wisdom dawned on me and I realised
That all men across the four oceans
Are all brothers in arms
In their eternal search for the elusive self

MYSTIC VEIL

The fiery quest for knowledge
Blazing in the intellectual cauldron
The icy mountain winds of vagueness
Chokes the yearning for creativity
The razing dust storm of doubts
Pouring uncertainty into eyes so wise
The supposedly unconditional love
Enmeshed in the web of expectations
The dimming glimmer of hope
Waiting for the hammer of enlightenment
To break the shackles of prejudicial learning

SEEKER

The path meanders through forests and deserts
I know not where I am going, like a blind traveller
I go on with my inquisitive walking stick
Searching for some elusive thing
My feet are sore, my heart is weak, and my vision is hazy
Many a wise man has invited me to join their chosen path
But I know not why I could not stop and rest
My journey will continue till I meet the truly enlightened
Who tells me that my search is futile and what I seek is not
there
For me to acquire but is already there in me to realize

REIGN OF THE SUBCONSCIOUS

The mind drifts and wanders
In the desert sand of competing ideas
Looking for the oasis under the cool shadows
Of palm trees made up of rhymes
The pen of thought involuntarily scratches
On the tabular rasa of intense emotions
The words pour out breaking the shackles
Of defined structures and frames of rules
To the utter surprise of my intellectual mind
As the subconscious ultimately takes the reins

PRISM

Unformed thoughts stirring in the subconscious
Like feathers swirling in the turbulent wind
The rainbow of varying thoughts
Reflected in the prism of the mind
Like the rays of the rising sun
The hidden meaning cuddles like an unborn child
Emerging within the womb of the consciousness
Waiting for the contractions of the mind
To bring out from the depths of my existential core
Into the new waking world
Of literary sunshine

UNFOLDING

The fire rages within, burning aside
The framework of poetic rules
Let critics mock my writing style
But with gay abandon my spirit roars
And rises into the sky
Towards an unlimited, unbound horizon
To choose from the wide spectrum of colours
To pour literary paint on the canvass of imagination
To the utter joy and delight
Of my unfolding inner self

STIRRINGS

Whether awake or asleep
The stirrings continue to churn
Within the core of the subconscious
Like a giant, awakening tsunami
Ready to break the boundaries
Unbinding the imagination
And uprooting routine themes
Causing untold agony to the words
Trying to push themselves out of the womb
Of the hazy mystic world of creation
Deep within, to come alive eventually
From the chaos that is the consciousness

IMAGINATION

The relentlessly rising waves of ideas
Breaking on the fertile shore of the mind
Forming a foam of floating words
The coiled serpent of intuition
From the deep chaotic sea within
Springing up to jolt one out of reverie
To give meaning and beauty
To the slow forming contours
Of my unbridled poetic imagination

GUIDE ME

The flames of passion dancing
Like the lightning in the dark sky
Licking the wounds of failure to capture
The spirit, radiance and beauty of her
With the eternally poised paintbrush
Waiting to dip into the richest colours
The white canvas fixed firmly on the easel
Looks mockingly at me
Oh! Spirit of Leonardo! Descend from heaven
Into my hand, and guide me as I paint Her

BLESS ME

Poetic urge like a coiled serpent waiting
For the lid of imagination to blow off
The fiery struggle within the depths
Of the volcanic molten lava of ideas
Struggling to erupt into lightning stanzas
Oh, Goddess Calliope! Let me be
Your eternally blessed disciple

(Calliope was the muse of epic poetry)

FLIGHT OF CREATIVITY

On the wings of imagination I soar into the sky of creativity
Fleeing from the shackles which have kept my spirit in captivity
The wide spectrum of feelings floating abundantly in nature
Giving my thoughts the edge I need to embark upon a joyful adventure
The flow of words merging into a beautiful theme
The meaning may not be clear to many but no one else is to blame
As I intend to present my inner self to readers in a decorative frame

RIVER OF POETRY

The eternal spring deep down in the unfathomable, subconscious well
Will not wait for some erudite savant to come and ring the bell
The unleashed, unchecked, pour of words pregnant with meaning
Flows ceaselessly, uncorrupted into the consciousness, unaware of any jarring
The golden path laid on the flowing river by the setting sun can be the way
The old woman with a wrinkled face and the crooked smile can also have a say
The mischievous, kind and enchanting smile of an innocent child
Or the shy glance of a newly married, blushing bride
For the searching poetic mind anything can act as a creative trigger
And will undoubtedly break through the grammatical banks and unleash the poetic river

POETIC GUIDANCE

Thoughts and feelings merging together in a flow, poetic
Sentences dancing and forming shapes utterly chaotic
No semblance of order or sense of rhythm visibly seen
But the instinct to write forcing me with intent so keen
Oh! Poets of the bygone eras, with your minds so imaginative
Guide me into making sense and pouring out something creative

PEACE

The soul searching for everlasting peace
 Traversing paths unknown
Seeking solace from those who claim enlightenment
Realizing that they are also mere travellers like oneself
But have covered more distance and gone down more paths
Is there anyone who is really enlightened,
Always in a state of constant peace and bliss?
Or is everyone like me, searching here and there
Sometimes attaining it and sometimes not?

URGE TO WRITE

Deep down in the heart, a ripple starts to emerge
The feelings and thoughts then collide with an imperative urge
To understand the meaning of the waves that slowly and steadily surge
There is complete vagueness, without any coherence
But slowly a shape, a form starts to form with some reverence
Which finally comes out from the heart as my pen's utterance

WORLDLY SELF

Running away from responsibilities and duties
May provide temporary respite but ultimately
There is no escape from them as there is no other alternative
The world, the situation, the circumstances will always change
And no one can hold them still for even a moment
The best way is to look into one's strengths and weaknesses
And work on them to improve oneself and reduce vulnerabilities
To cope with challenges head on
And with confidence, competence and a focused game plan

RAMBLINGS

Like thunder riding on the lightning
Feelings ride through my poems
Are they garbled or hazy I know not
To keep my sanity there is no alternative but to say
Whatever it is that I feel I must
Like mountains whose summits are covered in snow
The stanzas may have rhymes
Or like a lone camel in the sandy desert
The lines may be ambling
But they are invariably a part
Of my inner heart's pouring
As every word comes
Out of a great deal of struggling

CO-TRAVELLERS

The pleasure and pain, the agony and the ecstasy
The ups and downs, the peaks and troughs
The sweat, the blood, the bane and the boon
The supporting gestures and the scornful looks
The shower of praises and the burn of curses
In the walk of life these are our co-travellers
No one can walk alone on this long path
So they become our eternal companions

OUTPOURINGS

With the trident of feeling, word and sentence
I pierce the nebulous subconscious
To draw out the nectar of poetical meaning
As the outpourings of my inner heart's suffering
Then the dancing elves of stanzas emerge
To come alive in the poem into which they submerge

(Trident is the weapon of Sea God Poseidon)

URGE

On the wings of imagination my thoughts soar
The words and sentences, like a fountain from my pen pour
Hidden meanings like a string of pearls emerge
Feelings, thoughts, pain and joy finally converge
With the blessings of the poets from the past
A poem comes out of the womb of struggle at long last

FROM THE DEPTHS

As birds gather twigs to build their cosy golden nests
I gather words to give expression to this hazy mental mist
About the rules of the poetry I no longer seem to care
As raw emotions and feelings emerge from me to share
From deep down they surge and emerge, from my heart
And pour out for my readers and fans who appreciate art

EMPTY SPEECHES

Gnawing at my innards is the relentless hunger
Talk of freedom and liberty stokes my anger
The fools who give speeches from their ivory towers
Are they aware that poverty has vicious power?
Rolling in riches surrounded by luxuries all around
Their speeches sound to me like the bark of a bloodhound
Let them come out and try, even for a day, in ghettos to survive
Then I will resign and not allow my anger to live

THE MIND

Waves upon waves rising in the sea
Relentlessly moving to shoreline
Only to break and recede
Thoughts upon thoughts rising in the subconscious
And moving towards awareness
To cause pleasure, pain, hurt
Elation, joy, and despair
Oh, lost and wandering mind!
When will you learn to attain
The tranquillity of the deep blue sea?

QUEST

The wandering mind meanders
To the places unseen and unheard of
In its never-ending quest
For the true meaning of life
Tired and weary it comes back
To realize that the meaning
Lies within oneself

TREASURE

The search for the unknown treasure
The sight on a distant land
The preparation for the long journey
The fear of unknown dangers
The uncertainty of reaching the destination
Oh man of the material world
Why indulge in such a vain search
When you can look within yourself
And find the treasure buried inside

KNOWLEDGE

Browsing through the labyrinths of the world
With all the feelings wrapped up safely under guard
Is like wandering down the Library of Congress*
Deep in a miserable recess
The treasure trove available in those books
Can bring any wanderer back
From the nadir of unfathomable despair
And bestow the gift of boundless cheer

(* Biggest library in the world in Washington DC)

JUST AND FAIR

The sea laughing and pushing at the shore with its waves
Offering its wide open treasures to all and sundry
The wind flowing and touching
All the animate and inanimate without discrimination
The sun shining on the creeks and crevices
On the savants and the saints in equal measure
The earth offering its immense treasure troves
Of flora and fauna to all, unhesitatingly
Why doesn't man learn from the vast universe
To be just, fair and equitable?

Suffering

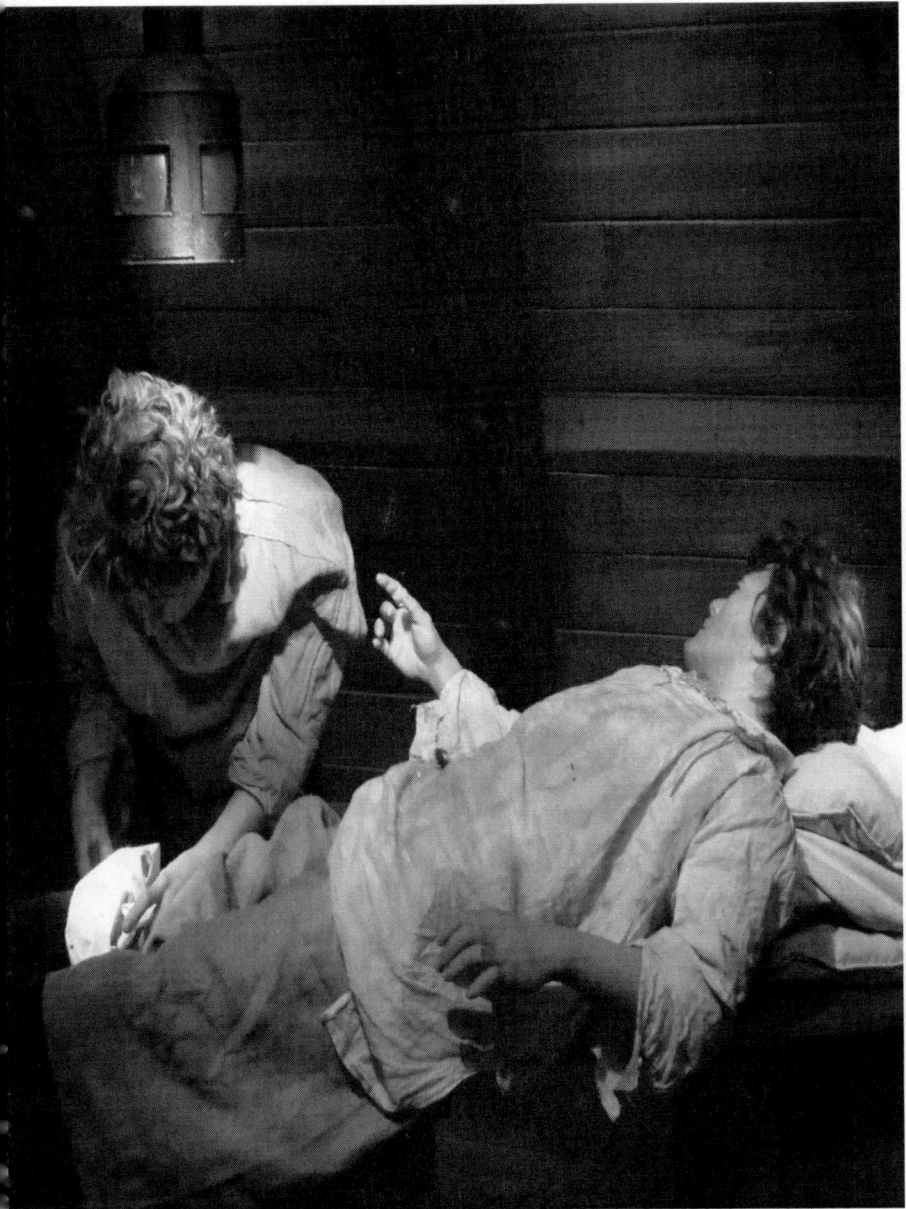

The path of sorrow,and that path alone
Leads to the land where sorrow is unknown
(William Cowper 1731-1800)

PEGASUS

The ever-burning desire
Leaving behind amber embers
The cry of the wounded
Unheard by the savage silence
The eternal rebel
Hiding behind impenetrable manners
The uncontrollable wildness
Held together by steel bands of mildness
The rawness of existence
Embellished by superficial artistry
Where have you gone,
My unbridled Pegasus?

(Pegasus: A winged horse in Greek Mythology)

ETERNAL QUESTION

The spring, the sunshine
The moonlight, the cool breeze
To whom they belong?
The sorrow, the suffering
The wounds, the scars
Who chooses to bear?
The heavenly, the divine
The blissful, the redeemed
Who are these blessed few?
The fearful, the cowering
The shaken, the forlorn
Who are those cursed souls?
Oh! Children of the Almighty
Why are you not all equal?

FOLLY

From time immemorial, the name of God has been misused
Abused by all and sundry in the struggle
For money, power and supremacy
The cunning and the arrogant have always made it a point
To scream the loudest, trying to assemble
The ignorant masses and forcing them to do their bidding
They defended their actions and desires
By quoting and citing examples from the sacred scriptures
The true meaning of which they barely comprehended
They flout their intolerance of other's beliefs and ideas
As proof of their deeply rooted convictions
Finally, mankind has succeeded in erasing
Even the last vestiges of the presence of a loving God
And the sanctity of the scriptures from innumerable religions

THE TRUE ONE

Despair paired with depression
Dragging me down into the abyss
The spirits forever haunting
The continuous soul-searching
Oh, the One true God,
When will you beckon to me
With the beacon of your blessings

LORD

The never ending agony
The ever lengthening path
The weakened limbs
The failing sight
The looming darkness
The hovering shadows
The frightening cry
Of the cowering lamb
Oh, Shepherd of all! When will you come back to us?

THE BEAST

The lurking, savage beast of evil thoughts
Ever hidden inside, with all its cunning
Its claws sharpened, waiting to pounce
And tear through the shroud of sanity
The chains of reason and the straps of determination
Holding the beast down
I wish for the power of knowledge and awareness
To give me more strength to hold the beast
Pinned down in its dungeon forever

DESPAIR

The pain of the prophets from different religions
Searing my shoulders as I carry it to different regions
The scriptures and the sayings of those great mentors
Don't make any difference to present day drifters
Nature, the stars and the planets cry in unison
Looking down at the materialistic world that lacks vision
Even if they descend to earth from their celestial abode
Can they really break the gripping, malicious mould?

LAZARUS

The deprived, enmeshed in endless agony
The eternal wait for the balm of bounty
The shattered dreams, pieces of broken glass
Reflecting the myriad motions of the multitude
The callous raven pecking at the wound
The unshed tears drying up in the pool
The sarcastic laughter of the satanic few
Searing the conscience of the silent
When will the Lazarus of the nameless masses
Wake up to the call of righteous activism?

(Lazarus - the brother of Mary Magdalene and Martha - was raised from the dead by Jesus after four days in the tomb)

ETERNAL WAIT

The cocoon of complacency dulls the finer senses of the youth
Wallowing in riches which provide security that is a myth
Their aim, purpose, and goals in life are lost in pursuit of worldly
pleasure
No benchmark, no ideal, no higher principle to measure
Drugs push the young to the depths of depravity and despair
Struggling with themselves to retake their sanity unimpaired
Waiting for the enlightened Master to come to the rescue and
begin to repair

APOCALYPSE

The never falling raindrops
The patchy arid desert
The sunken pale cheeks
The hollow burning eyes
The invisible empty belly
The bare bent vertebrae
The unsatisfied evil blade
Forever painted in red
Oh, mannequins pretending to be men!
Are you so manacled by your programming
That you continue to be mute spectators
To the march of the Four?

(The Four Horsemen of the Apocalypse)

CRY

The tortured, twisted and suffering souls crying for redemption

The sins of the past haunting without mercy or exemption

The agony of the cry from the inky depths of darkness emerging

Appealing to the higher Gods for their help but they aren't budging

The desperate cries failing to pierce the stony Gods, who won't be listening

The deep suffering of the soul, mercilessly into pits submerging

Oh, God! Why delay in descending, when the hope of humanity is waning

HEALTH CARE FOR POOR

(Poem dedicated to President Obama for introducing
Affordable Care Act in USA)

The tired, the sick, the old, the downtrodden and the poor; who cares for them all?

To be sophisticated, powerful, rich and famous with a luxury boat in tow

Allowing the poor to live in misery and not responding to their call

Where is the time, patience and empathy that the fabulously rich ought to know?

Is it imperative to have a rebellious uprising to make them realize

That they are also children of God and have an equal right to rise?

DRUMS

The beating of drums
Urging the under-privileged
To march against the oppression
By the oligarchy
The thundering sounds
Made by the marching feet
Shake the foundations
Of this fortress of cruelty
The inevitable triumph
Of right over wrong
Visible to all those
Who can read the writing on wall?
You power hungry monsters
When are you going
To recognize the truth
Of your impending doom

COCOON

The blanket of complacency
Keeping warm the yawning Yin
Ennui, the eternal devil, casting
A shadow on the Sisyphean spirit
The wings of creativity singed
By the storm of stifling silence
Oh! My little butterfly
When will you come out of your cocoon?

FURY

The facade of confidence buffeted by the arrogance
Crumbling against the wrath and fury of the suffering
Exploited, downtrodden, vulnerable poor
Will it be possible for the virtue and wisdom of a few surviving sane
To hold up the dam of logical reasoning and righteous anger
Against the fury of the many, to save the megalomaniacal and rich few
Will the wisdom of sages and savants enlighten these selfish creatures,
To share their riches for the benefit of all?

CRUMBS OF BREAD

The coiled serpent of agony raising its head
For the inevitable fight for crumbs of bread
There are lots of people like the French Queen
But there is no justice that can take away their sheen
People struggle to create immense national wealth
Looters and cheaters are there to steal it by stealth
When will they face the angry guillotine of people's wrath?

(When people were suffering for lack of bread, the Queen, Marie Antoinette, allegedly said "Let them eat cake")

LEGACY

The devil of Greed, relentlessly riding the selfish horse
Fleecing the fleeing innocent without an iota of remorse
Wanton destruction of God-given bountiful natural resource
Not allowing anyone to let life run its natural course
Depleting the strength and boundless beauty of mother Earth
Being the cause of natural calamities not being given enough thought
When will we learn the lessons from the unforgiving past?
Is all we're leaving to posterity nothing but chaos and unrest?

DANCING DEVIL

The unending agony seeping through the body and the heart
The final unspoken word on the lips, ready to be uttered
The magic of love burnt into ashes and lying scattered
The wreckage of happiness's ship floating in a salty sea of tears
The devil of drugs coursing through the body of my lover
Can I utter the bond-breaking goodbye forever?
To him who was once my heart and soul
Who is now only a human being in shape but a devil in truth
Laughing at me and stabbing me with words and deeds

(Dedicated to all those struggling to free from abusive relationships)

FIGHT AGAINST TERROR

Terrorists without a morsel of conscience cause a bomb blast
The series of bombs planted by these fanatics explode so fast
They take a toll on God-given human life at an immeasurable cost
Why are these cruel, vengeful people fighting for a cause already lost?
Irrespective of beliefs, all should combine their efforts, which is a must
To fight these evil people, whose brains are beginning to rust
And ensure that their future plans, to wreck human life, turn to dust

SWIMMING ALONE

In the ocean of life, I swim alone
Powerful sharks and wealthy whales
Are out there in the open, hunting
Waiting to sink their sharp teeth into me
To suck my virginal blood and let out a howl
Of victory over the unsuspecting me
I swim towards an old fisherman
With a wrinkled, weather-beaten face
Mistaking him to be wise, I swim
Only to receive a nasty poke
I swim far away feeling lonely
Till I saw other lonely women like me
Swimming but holding on to an invisible safety net
Of sharing, secure in their sisterhood
Now I swim alone but never feel lonely
As they are for me and I am for them

(Dedicated to all women who faced sexual harassment)

TORMENTOR

Who is he who torments and tortures me,
With the brutal abuse on my body and soul?
My shell and my mind become
Numb and dull with the unbearable pain
As he unleashes his merciless physical and verbal threats
The beatings, the bruises, on my body and soul becomes
Unbearable, as a living hell is created here and now
How is it that I loved this person so dearly once
And never thought of leaving him till the end?
How is it that the light of my life and the wonder of my eyes
Has turned into a beast, savage beyond redemption?
Oh! Drugs of Satan!
What have you done to my dearest one?

MY MIGHTY MIND

Agony and suffering, suffering and agony
Cruel fate with its bloodthirsty sword
Cut through the lifelines of my broken body
Making me a cripple and a quadriplegic
Confirmed to the square metre of wheelchair
My broken body strapped as I struggle to break free
My imagination soars like an emboldened eagle
But my body has shrivelled up like a mummy

In the wonderland of my fantasy world
I gather broken branches and fallen leaves
Like a gay grasshopper gathering its tunes
To be poured eventually out of my inner self

The ideas, the words, come like a torrential rain
With the pen in my mouth I write on the paper
Of my imagination, fixed on the easel
Of perseverance, to prove the might of my mind

(Dedicated to all Quadriplegics)

AM I A CASTAWAY?

Why do these people laugh at and mock my gait?
I know I'm not like them and can't walk as straight
My voice sounds like musical notes but they call it sissy
I don't know why they are being so fussy
They are so ignorant of the Chinese concept of Yin and Yang
Always bullying me like some uncouth, troublesome gang
Everyone is special and unique in one way or the other
But their mob mentality teaches them to make fun of me rather
Why should I conform as I want to live my own way?
What right have they to treat me like some castaway?

OH FATHER

Oh, Father! Why have you abandoned me?
On the hot desert sand, I walk along with my son
Searching for the oasis, but mirages are calling to me
To come and quench my thirst
My search for the palm tree to provide shade for my son
Has only led to shrubs full of thorns
I know I have committed a mistake in not following your advice
But cannot you forgive and get my youthful folly
And be there for me in my hour of need?
In my never-ending journey with my son on my shoulders
To find a shade to rest under, and an a oasis to quench my thirst
Father, are you there with me?

SOUNDS OF SILENCE

Sounds, sounds, a million sounds
Of the ringing of church bells
Of the flapping of a bird's wings
Of the waves hitting the sandy beach
Of the laughter of a happy child
Of the cry of a little baby
Of the murmurings of an old woman
Of the march of uniformed soldiers
Of the sound of rapid gunfire
Of the clanking of moving tanks
Of the moan of a wounded soldier
Of the wails of starving orphans
When will the world understand
The beauty of the sound of silence?

SILENCE

The deafening sound of silence
Is the death knell to the dance of sound
Pouring from the soul, pricked
By the sharpened beaks of insensitive eagles
Adding fuel to the outwardly calm sea of fiery stirrings
Buffeted by the winds of desire
Filling up every crevice in the heart
Beware, oh creative mind, of silence
Which is sharper than noise
As it can shred apart your innermost poise

PHOENIX

The beatings, the bruises and the tears
The torture, agony and the suffering
The shackles of simmering hatred
The baloney from the barbaric, urbane few
The never-yielding spirit
And the sense of hope that never dies
Oh, my poor fellow sufferers!
Rise like the phoenix from the ashes
And fly to your undiscovered heights

IS IT WORTH IT?

At the confusing crossroads I stand
To the left is the road to power
To the right is the one leading to Mammon
Straight ahead is the road paved with gold, leading to Hell
At my back is the road full of thorns, leading to Heaven
I know not how I have reached this crossroads
I remember losing something to gain something else
But now if I do not know what I lost or what I gained
Then does this struggle hold any meaning? I know not!

MASK

Different hues, different shapes
Different material, different designs
So many masks we carry
To wear at religious functions
To wear at raves
To wear when we're with the boss
To wear when with our wives
To wear when we're with a mistress
To wear when we're with our parents
To wear around our children
Which one is the real me?
The dividing line between
The wearer and the mask
Slowly melts away what's real
Until I eventually become
Nothing but a multi-faceted mask

HIS HOLINESS

Like a ray of the sun piercing through the darkness
There emerged a blessed one full of holiness
The simple ways in which He chooses to live
Immeasurable happiness to his disciples does it give
For all those suffering, He is a beacon Of Hope
The present shepherd of Rome, the people's Pope

(An Ode to the present Pope)

Companionship

Companionship:Phtograph taken by Author in Kukenhof Amsterdam

There are wonders in true affection: It is a body of enigma,mystery,and
Riddles;wherein two become one
as they both become two Images
(Sir Thomas Brown 1605-1682)

RENDEVOUZ

What a dilemma, to choose or not to choose
Is the decision going to be wise or unwise?
I have seen her and part of me is no doubt impressed
And I doubt any of her failings she has suppressed
I have bared my heart and my mind before her
What she thinks of me now I am not sure
The outcome of our pre-arranged first date
I am sure will affect our joined fate
Standing at the crossroads, my love is at stake
Oh, God, in your infinite wisdom please give me a break

FOREVER

Forever for you my dear love I will wait
Cyclones may come and take everything away with a sweep
But I will wait for you as it is my love's trait
Others may think differently and may weep
But the hope in my heart springs eternal
That fate will favour our love for each other
As I know the desire for you is not simply carnal
But a purer love, to be with you, together forever

MY HONEY DEW

You
My love,
I definitely knew
Were my honey dew
Girls like you are rare
Leaving you makes my heart tear
I will always be there for you
Come whatever, moments without you will be few
Together we will swim the ocean of this turbulent life
As I know you are destined to be my wife

ENTREATY

In the moonless night, in the darkness visible
Oh my darling let us play hide and seek
In the misty mountains, at the forgotten altar
Let us pray together to the unknown gods

In the majestic mountains, in the crystal clear water
Of gurgling creeks, let us swim with gay abandon
In the garden of evergreen leaves and perpetually blooming flowers
Let us dance to the tunes of the whispering winds

On the cusp of the crescent moon, under the light
Of the sparkling stars, in the midst of dancing elves
Oh my dearest love let us take our eternal vows
To love each other and live together until death do us apart

WIFE

Ever-patient ears
Forever beaming smile
An understanding heart
A gentle caring touch
Genuinely warm hug
An unspoken word
Eloquently expressed
Would I be what I am now?

LIGHT OF MY HEART

The sound of footsteps
Echoes in my fluttering heart
The whiff of fragrance
From your rustling dress
Carried by a gentle, passing wind
Eyes pouring an unspoken love
As the never-forgotten hugs
Gently generate warmth
The heart speaks
From the depths of despair
Oh, light of my heart!
When will you alight?

TO BE WITH YOU

Let us dance to the furious tunes of winds whirling
To the guttural howling sounds of the tornado twisting
Let us ride the dark clouds brandishing streaks of lightning
And get drenched in the torrential rain's outpouring
Let us together travel to the ends of the world magical
With you I promise to always be loving and reverential

JOURNEY

Let us ride together on the clouds of happiness
Let us find our way through the forest of trials and tribulations
Let us walk through the deserts of pain and agony
Let us wade through the oceans of elation and ecstasy
Hand-in-hand let us walk together
On the meandering path of life's journey
Let us stay together till death do us part
And eventually face the inevitable
With the comfort of me being there for you
And you being there for me, with smiles on our faces

WILL YOU BE THERE?

Will you be there to catch me
When I fall from the yonder blue sky?
Will you be there at the bottom of the sea
When I feel myself being pulled in too deep?
Will you be there when I get burned
And depend on a machine for my survival?
Will you be there when I am on the top floor
About to jump to my death?
Promise me that you will always be there
For all the journeys in my life
To always catch me when I fall

NEVER

The mountains may break
And fall into the oceans
The Earth may stand still
And the universe may cease all motion
The sun may self-combust
And burn away everything in its path
The devil may descend
To put obstacles in my way
Angels may fly down
With blessings to lure me away
But remember, my love
I never will from you break away

DAUGHTER

My princess, I was holding the beauty of the world
When I took you into my arms when you were born
The little steps you took, hesitatingly
Shook the bottom of my heart, especially when you fell
As you grew, I experienced the blooming
Of different seasons, days and nights,
When you wanted to start your own nest,
It pained me let you go create your own little world
Remember my precious, whether you are four,
Fourteen or forty, I will always be there for you

MOTHER'S LOVE

Mother's love is like a wonderfully woven blanket
A single hug and a smile makes all sorrows perish
When she's gone, there's always a spot in your life that feels vacant
Memories of her will always linger, for us to cherish

MY LOVE

We may stay apart for some time or forever live together
But I pledge to you my love, which will never wither
The dark clouds of doubt may sometimes largely loom
Soothsayers may predict for our love eternal doom
Deep down in my heart I always know, my dearest love
However mighty they may be, from either earth or heaven
My steady love for you, try as they might, will never, change

Experience and wisdom

We learn wisdom from failure Much more than from Success,
we often discover What will do,by finding out What will not do,and
Probably he who never made a mistake never made a discovery
(Samuel Smiles 1812-1904)

THOUGHTS

Wild horses are like thoughts unbridled
With logic and introspection they have to be saddled
If actions are carried out without restraining thought
One will end up like a piece of metal wrought
Remember that most feelings are thought-based
Control those thoughts and the negative feelings will be erased

PAUSE

Would you like to immerse yourself in the sound of silence?
It will definitely reveal to you life's essence
The world is filled with cacophonous noises
And has its own Babel tower full of voices
In the vast universe of beauty, rhythm and space
Why does one struggle to rise, without any trace of remorse?
Pause in your mad and morbid race with time
Only then will you find the beauty in Nature's rhyme

NEVER LEAVE

Climb the tallest mountain
Swim the turbulent seas
Explore every meandering path
Discover the end of a rainbow
Catch a cloud and pin it down
Hold a moonbeam in your hand
Make the sunshine your halo
Follow your dreams for as long as you live
Pursue them no matter what others may say

RITUALS

We know that eventually all of us will turn into dust
So we enjoy all the carnal pleasures as if it is a must
Though we believe that we should have in God full trust
We allow our inner spiritual spark to gather dust
Though all the wisdom of scriptures is available in a gist
We sink into the mundane, meaningless, ritualistic mist

FLOW

Life is like the flow of a river
The water is same but the drops are all different
Be what you are and regret it never
Live each moment of your life in the present

ENNUI

Ennui the ever-present shadow
Enveloping the invisible spirit
Clouding ever-active young minds
Pushing them in the path of
Never-ending thrills
Of rave, rap, rhapsody
Oh my restless evergreens
Why don't you pause for a while?
Only to reflect that there never can be
An eternal magic spell
Every peak rises by the side of a nadir
Every success is shadowed by a failure
Every pleasure is preceded by a pain
The triumph and the travails
The roughs patches and troughs
Are all part of life's continuum

VALOUR

Realize that courage is not like a solid rock
In the face of adversity it evaporates like camphor
Make concerted efforts to come out of the shock
That is the definition of true valour

JOURNEY

Success or failure doesn't matter
As long as your success
Doesn't go to your head nor failure
Make you drown in sorrows
The goal itself is not as important
Try to enjoy the journey
The ups and downs along with way
As the goal posts will go on changing

AVATAR

The emotional threads of life are like an unstrung guitar
Bring them together and tune them like proper strings
You will realise the benefits of assuming a new avatar
And relish the melodious tranquillity it brings

MISSED MOMENTS

Time is like the eternal flow of a river
A moment missed is lost forever
Every moment is like a shining gem
So do not walk around with an expression so glum

POETIC STRUGGLE

The words and sentences of unwritten poems
Dance in my dreams forming different rhymes
From the unfathomable depths of unknown understanding
The formless sentences struggle to find their different meanings
The words and sentences change like the shifting sands in desert
When formed rhythmically, they sound like a melodious concert
As the rays of the early morning sun pierce through clouds
The poems emerge from the middle of these mysterious shrouds
In the early brilliance of dawning light, I grab pen and paper
As any delay in putting these words down will make them disappear like vapour

BEING POETIC

I catch the sword of lightning to slice through the sky
To enable my unfettered imagination to fly
To unknown heights my creativity will reach
The words full of meaning that will subtlety teach
The elves and fairies which float in the heavenly air
Will take the nib of my pen and bless it with literary flair
To the end of my journey through poetic sight I write
That the world of poets will read them with delight

PAST

Do you feel like the past is an ever-creeping shadow,
Following you like a faithful dog wherever you go?
Would you even exist without the past or is it just a myth?
Is it the past that shapes your present
And, eventually, your future?
Can we forget the past and live in the present?
As the wise men say live in present
As the present becomes the past
And shapes your future
Can we unshackle ourselves from the chains
Of the misery, hurt and pain of the past
So that our present can have unblemished moments?
And can we live fully with the awareness
That those moments will ultimately shape our future
Giving mankind the confidence
To create a better future through their efforts?

FEELINGS

Different patterns, colours, textures and threads are feelings
Woven and spread in the mind like a carpet full of meanings
Difficult it is to gauge the depth and width of these emotions
As they churn and come out with the intensity of the oceans
To have, hold, and control them is undoubtedly difficult
Restraining and analysing them is the only way as there is no shortcut

POWER OF KNOWLEDGE

Wise men always say acquire knowledge as knowledge is power
Acquiring knowledge without putting it to use is like an empty shower
Being known as an erudite scholar by reading a number of books
And trying to keep the knowledge to yourself is not the way it works
With the knowledge acquired, doing something practical for humanity
Is the way to gain stature and respect in your community
Be proactive to constructively implement your ideas
Then everyone will look at you as the person with touch of Midas

ANGER

It burns like hot coals,
Leaving a scar on your soul
Like a ripple in the pond, it rises from the subconscious
Uncontrolled, like a tidal wave it can become very vicious
The first step to take is to understand the source
And taking actions to control it, to end up without remorse
The best way is to analyse the feelings and be not reactive
With logical, rational thinking, and an open mind be proactive

SANE ADVICE

The words I am writing now try always to remember
When facing difficulties one has to be strong like timbre
One may face a number of ups and downs in daily life
But one should be in a position to live without much strife
Conflict, pain, sorrow, joy, excitement you cannot from life shut
Use them all, balance them with equanimity, as there is no shortcut
Cursing someone else and blaming fate will not do you any good
To realize that all the answers lie within you is to be shrewd

DEEDS

Most people are under the impression that life is a mystery
You will realize that there is no such thing, if you go through history
Birth, growth, death are things which for everyone is inevitable
But the way you live your life should not be ordinary and forgettable
It is not the power, position and wealth which ultimately matter
What are important are your actions and deeds which make a few lives better
The footprints you leave on the sands of time will inevitably fade
The deeds you have done will linger in the memory of people, like precious jade

EMOTIONS

Like sharpened arrows, remarks some people will throw
They pierce and hurt you and wipe out your confident glow
Your ego and self-esteem will undoubtedly get a beating
To survive and prosper you have to deal without berating
The more emotional you are, the words will be more vicious
The scars left unattended will cause damage more poisonous
Do not absorb the unwarranted criticism like a soft sponge
Analyse them, counter them, or reject them, like an enlightened protégé

DREAMS

Like a thin vapour cloud of myriad colours it floats in your mind
Rising from the churning of unresolved conflicts just to unwind
You will sleep like an innocent child if they are sweet
And feel as if they are made exclusively for you as a special treat
Sometimes they are so horrible and bad, that in dreams you shiver
An the next promising day is spoiled as memories linger
Do not give any importance or significance to these dreams
As they are just unresolved feelings coming out like small streams
Rush not to dream interpreters for the so-called inner meaning
Meditate and strengthen your belief in God to stop them from troubling

MENTOR

Do not allow your mind to be idle or let it gather dust
Regular sharpening and removing all cobwebs from the mind is a must
Otherwise there is an absolute possibility of it going to rust
You should have a mentor who will be just
As you know that when dealing with the problems of life there is no rest
To succeed in life you should have in your mentor full trust
Having Him lead you down your path will make you feel less lost
The knowledge and experience He has you should use most
And his continuous guidance will enable you to pass every test
All that I have said to my young friends should not be taken in jest

MOODS

Like currents, from the depths of the ocean these moods surface
Turbulent, calm, or choppy there will never be a warning preface
Not only will they upset your balance but also your near and dear
Be careful early on and try to understand them without fear
Remember, moods are mostly feelings based on thought
Try to understand, analyse and block negative thinking's onslaught
Then you will definitely end up being calmer and less distraught

TWIN DEVILS

Of devils there are two
Which exist just to torment mankind
Regret about the past
And worry about the future put you in bind
Regretting for days
About past mistakes that will not alter
Better learn from these mistakes
So as not to again falter
Worrying about what will happen
In some distant future
Will not alter it
But will put you in a mental torture
Think and prepare for the unforeseen
Strategize, organize and plan
Then the worry will definitely disappear
And you can face future with élan

BEING AWARE

The whisper of the elves dancing and floating in the air
The laughter of the lovely nymphs riding on the waves
The fragrance of a single rose in a garden full of flowers
Broken glass turning a single ray of the sun into a million colours
The innocent, lovely smile of a child sleeping in its mother's lap
The rustle of dried leaves falling from the branch of a mighty tree
The buzz of the ever busy bees roaming around and collecting honey
The grace of the enlightened guru pouring forth from his beaming smile
The warmth of a gentle hug from a compassionate and loving mother
Live life fully, being aware of the small wonders which are around you

BALANCE

In today's world, it's easier to be a sinner than a saint
To be a saint you cannot have heart which is faint
Only thing you can do is turn into a sinner
 And wallow in the pseudo-happiness of a front runner
It's when you stop running that the sins will come to catch
Just as wise men say, you will never be out of their reach
To eventually end up as decent human being
You have to minimize the sins committed and have virtues aplenty

SEARCH

The eternal search for the secret of life
Has continued for ages with a lot of strife
What is it, knowledge, wealth, beauty or valour?
Scholars have given it different hues and colours
But failed to fully understand the substance
Of its unknown hidden essence
When will they realize that there is no gem hidden?
That life should be lived as you wish before it become leaden

LOOK INSIDE

Rumblings are heard from unknown depths
The waves of love, anger, pity, hate rise from within
The beauty and ugliness as seen in the world
Are nothing but reflections of the inner self
So stop playing the blame game
And look inwards to change, instead
Of expecting the world to change to suit you

REALISE

The pain and agony of the soul, fettered and tortured
The scars from the fanatics as their teachings uttered
The supposed authoritative interpretation of the scriptures
Causing hatred and making brothers fight like vultures
Forgotten are the common threads of the spiritual carpet
Despite the savants blowing wisdom's trumpet
When humans cease their petty squabbles
They will walk hand-in-hand into God's own portal

SALVATION

The cobwebs of illogical and blind superstition
Rational thinking should slice through like Katana
The world needs wise men that move without trepidation
To create from chaotic disorder a blissful nirvana
Only then can there be salvation for the innocent believers
From the charlatans who form a tribe of great deceivers

(Katana: A sword used by Japanese Samurai Warriors)

JADED VIEW

The lurking green monster
Forever festering and trying to foster
Evil thoughts mocking the glory of another
Which makes your affection for him wither
Reflect and realize that you are a unique feather
Which can firmly withstand all sorts of weather
You should be floating on your own cloud of dreams
Without letting yourself drown in jealous streams

DREAMS TO PURSUE

Pursue your dreams with vigour unfettered
People around you may say a hundred things
To make your mind confused and cluttered
But be aware that dreams will come true
Only when you are truly and fully focused
Study, plan and be completely committed
And move towards your chosen path with dedication
Your will power will definitely take you
To your dream destination, without complication

TEACHINGS

The true character of a person lies in differentiating
The wheat from the chaff, and the two isolating
The language used by mystics is undoubtedly esoteric
But the philosophy they preach is essentially dynamic
Which if practiced will save the world from a time chaotic
One has to escape the false prophet's rhetoric
Which promises to make one's rise to heaven meteoric

SMILE BACK

When the going gets tough, do not despair, smile back
When people criticise you, do not fight, smile back
When your love deserts you, do not get dejected, smile back
When someone hurts you, do not be depressed, smile back
When instead of shower of favours you get curses, smile back
Life is but a continuum of ups and downs, showers and flowers
It is your attitude and your will to face the situation that matters
As you are the captain of your ship of life, with the rudder in your hand
Just remember to smile back when death finally knocks at your door

WORDS AND DEEDS

The name, fame, wealth or power
Do not really matter
For when the time comes
All of them will falter
The theories, the stories,
The promises made, the assurances given
Remember, if they are not translated
Into action, you are never really forgiven
A single deed of kindness to the needy
Definitely will have more impact
Than a hundred words which you retract
Leave behind the platitudes and false utterances
And live solely through kind deeds and actions

MASTERING EMOTIONS

Most emotions are like an unbridled horse
Using them without caution will end up in remorse
To channel them properly is not an easy task
But to suppress them and act is like wearing a mask
Our emotions seem like they rise like waves of heat
But if we look carefully they are based on thought
Exercise control over the way thoughts form
Then you will be the master of your emotional dam

TOWER OF BABEL

Through the mass of humanity I walk alone
In the cacophony of voices mine isn't one
In the Tower of Babel I keep silent
I take up no arms in a world already violent
Though I am put down I keep my spirit high
I will not be stopped though many may try
Am I abnormal, special, or peculiar?
I know not but it is what I am proud to be

SAINT AND SATAN

Both Satan and the Saint undoubtedly in us reside
Which one comes out depends on what we decide
Constant introspection of values and attitudes, with vigilance
Will help one to attain, in the course of time, a sort of balance
Satan will be tamed as no one will be able to successfully remove
And the saint in you will be reflected in your actions, as you move

JANUS

The forces of Good and Evil are in constant battle
Which definitely makes your conscious mind rattle
The Savage and the Saint within you co-exist
In critical times, one emerges triumphant from the mist
Who will come, subjugating the other, depends on your maturity
And to achieve this, fill your body, mind and spirit with purity

PLAIN TRUTH

The speeches of the mystic will always be in an esoteric language
And appear to uninitiated or uninterested as garbage
But once one listens with interest and attention
The meaning of the words will remain in the mind for retention
Nothing secret or hidden, as these sayings are life's truth
And these teachings are both for elders and the youth
Like loving others selflessly, helping the needy
That too with devotion, humility and care, without being greedy

TORTOISE

A shell full of thoughts and feelings
We carry like a tortoise
Moving slowly and at the slightest hint of danger
Withdraw into this shell
With great hesitation we put
Our head outside and sensing calm again
Venture out with our tiny little steps
Thinking that the shell will always be there
To protect us, without realizing
That we carry an underbelly of untold vulnerabilities

LIFEBOAT

Sailing solo in a boat meant for one through the ocean of life
The waves of experience taking it up and down
The multitude of sea creatures
With different hopes and expectations
Brushing up against the boat
Then wandering off in different directions
The sails of reason are buffeted by emotional winds
The unfailing spirit of the lone sailor
Directing his boat in his journey to unknown destinations

DIVINE DANCE

Celebrate every moment of life with a joyful dance
The Almighty has given you everything you require as a gift
Always put in your best and do not leave anything to chance
And in the sea of struggle, your lifeboat will never be adrift

BOUNCE

Even with all your efforts, realize that you may fail
Because there's no point in ruing it all year long
Learn from your mistakes, come out of misery hale
Bounce back and sing the victory song

THE VOICE

The pride, the prejudice
The wealth, the arrogance
The beauty, the vanity
The strength, the stubbornness
The erudition, the mockery
Stop preening
In your vain glory
And listen to the gentle voice
Of the Almighty!

WIT

Know that humour will definitely enliven any group
But understand that your wit should not cause hurt
Otherwise your effort to create laughter will flop
Instead of creating unpleasantness, keep your mouth shut

BEACON

True knowledge is like a powerful beam
It cuts through the shackles of an ignorant mind
The intellect thus sharpened will then gleam
And the secret to success you will then find

SERENITY

Learn to take life a little less seriously and learn how to joke
Otherwise you may end up with a paralytic stroke
The strain of the ups and downs will make you crack
Unless you are wise enough to get back the serenity you lack

WISDOM

Why don't you stop playing this endless game?
And for your follies reassigning all blame
To take responsibility for them is your shame
Let them help you try and re-light wisdom's inner flame

Old age & death

Gather ye rose-buds while ye may Old times is still a-flying;
And this same flower which smiles today
Tomorrow will be dying
(Robert Henrick 1591-1674)

BUDDHAHOOD

Living fully in the present
Moving from moment to moment
Unaffected by the flow of events
And all the passing comments
Allows an individual
To find their centre
And eventually leads them
To a state of bliss known as Budhahood

INHERITED WISDOM

I carry with me the age-old wisdom of our forefathers
These wise words, which aren't of use to anyone right now
As all they want is life on a soft bed full of fragrant petals
These truths are not even subject to their consideration
False promises of riches, power and position are what appeal to them.
And the essence of the wisdom I have to present
Is the burden and agony we always carry as grownups
Which our fathers before us carried
When we were young and committing blunders

AGEING

Ageing is a process which is undoubtedly inevitable
The days spent as a youth are definitely unforgettable
The eyes become weak, the joints painful as the steps falter
The worldly possessions no longer matter
The memories of departed at faraway places linger
The spirit which once soared high becomes a little less strong
The issue is whether to grow up and behave with a gentle grace
Or become a garrulous, troublesome and cantankerous menace

TEMPLAR

The sayings of savants and scholars
Will definitely have a positive influence
Wise is the one who generously draws
From the confluence of the best of such thoughts
Acting on them with purpose
Depending on the situation is definitely wise
To proceed by ignoring such age-old advice
Will undoubtedly and inexorably lead one
In the direction of a grave full of follies
Discard such narrow modes of thinking
And put into practice the advice of scholars
You are sure to court blessed success
Like in the good old times did valiant Templars

(Templars are saintly warriors who used to protect travellers
going to Jerusalem during the Crusades)

THREE STAGES

The ghosts, the goblins, the trolls
All come out to haunt me in my dream
Cowering, I hide in a blanket roll
But the sweat pours out like a stream

Will she say yes, will she say no?
The nagging doubt gnaws at my mind
Can I survive a flat refusal?
Will I lose faith in all the mankind?

The twin devils of disease and decease
Staring and coming closer as I grow old
The fading memories pass through like a breeze
As the flicker of life loses its final hold

SUFFERING

The agony as I witness the suffering of my dear one
Makes me cry and breakdown with fear alone
My heart is like an ocean filled with unshed tears
As I know not when this perpetual pain will clear
With the love and commitment I carry for her
Can I not magically make the pain disappear?
God, tell me what is the purpose of my living
When I cannot do anything to alleviate her suffering?

TEARS

The relentless march of time
Gnawing at the vitality of youth
The unending flow of deep despair
Wrenched from fathomless vulnerability
From the twin pools of eyes
The god-given liquid pearls
Slowly moving like a rivulet
Down the reddened, pale cheeks
Dropping like red hot lava
Onto the heaving heart
Full of indelible images
Of the long-forgotten past
The yearning and the anguish
For so-called sweet nothings
And secretly stolen ethereal touches

LOSS OF A MOTHER

Suffering we saw you bear with grit,
Being unable to do much except watch
The ever-hovering, pitiless shadow
Tried our best to make you hale and hearty again
Our humble efforts you could but only grin and bear
Unsure we became of our childish endeavours
As with tears in our eyes we watched you fade
Joining our hands and stopping our hearts from breaking
As all our prayers could not make you stay
Knowing well that for each of us you did your best
We knelt before God Almighty to ask
To beg His blessings for your eternal rest

MOVE ON

Move on with your wonderful life
You may undoubtedly face the occasional strife
Be like a butterfly, moving from flower to flower
Don't be like the unborn baby, stuck in its cocoon forever

Do not forget every moment is a God -given gift
Be wary of allowing even a single minute to drift
Cut your umbilical cord, tied to the feet of Mammon
Fly like a possessed Pegasus to heights beyond

ROUND THE BEND

The cycle of life and death continues eternally, never coming to an end

Few faultlessly make the journey

From this end going round the bend

One comes out crying at the beginning to leave his mark early

In the process of his journey, he may succeed and create a cult

Or may fail to make one, his presence never felt

As he approaches the other end, grows the feeling of emptiness

Making him forget all the little things he's done with great happiness

Life is to be lived fully and passionately, making mistakes without regret

As one life ends the other life begins, which is realized by only a few I'll bet

STAGE

As the years pass by, the story of life unfolds
From the cradle, moving towards the grave
Full of myriad colours, touched by an unknown brush
With funny characters and sometimes ones not as funny
They pass through the stage, some joking and playing
Some laughing or crying
Some lost in thought
And some on a somnambulistic walk
All playing their brief roles on the stage
Who knows their purpose, or why they appear
Who knows to which netherworld they disappear!
Thoughts and feelings eternal
In the cauldron of consciousness crying to be heard
By whom? And for what? Who knows!

DREAMS

The dreams and desires
The wishes and hopes
The worries and concerns
Oh evergreen young ones
Remember, the time passes
Ending up with your memories
Gradually fading away
Like a Pebble on the riverbed
Slowly being eroded by the passing waters
Life turns into a worn-out clock
The hands of time moving slowly out of tune
Waiting for the inevitable halt

ANGUISH

From the depth of some unfathomable despair
Emerges the cry full of unimaginable anguish
Are you there? Are you with me?
The body is failing, the eyes are becoming misty
The limbs are loose and the steps are faltering
The halo of prestige and fame is slowly fading
Past sins are stalking the shadows like Satan
I am left in the abyss of loneliness
With withering desire and hope, can't continue my journey
Oh, God! Will you be there in my hour of need?

MEMORY

What does it mean
To be a human being?
Is it our body?
Is it our consciousness?
Or is it our feelings?
I know not!
Nothing more than a bundle
Of the feelings and emotions, which are all stored
In layers upon layers of memory
Once we sleep, there is no more
Of you or me, except vague dreams
And that tentative thread of our subconscious
Linked to our bodies in repose
Slowly you wake up
And the memory begins to fade
Wipe out these memories
And you are no longer you
Only your shell of a body remains
And who once was no longer is

(Dedicated to all those who suffer from Alzheimer's disease)

THE PATH

The far, ominous cry shattering the silence of the night
The never-ending pain piercing a fearful heart
The trials and tribulations liquefying into unshed tears
The path twists through the arid desert of doubts
Through the dense, dark clouds of confusion
Through the mass of mammon worshippers
My feet are sore, my body is withering
My spirit is dimming with this long, twisting journey
Oh, God Almighty! In your all-encompassing compassion
Why have you not laid out a straighter path to your heavenly
abode?

THE CRY

Unknown fears, haunting
And gnawing at all that is vital
The hope diminishing
The spirit yielding
The darkness closes in
Covering me like a mystic shroud
The awareness of the eternal soul
Trying to pierce through the armour
To touch my inner, tranquil core
At the moment of my final judgement
Will you be there to hold my hand,
My beloved saviour?

SALVATION

Youth, fading and forgotten
Resilience, bare and broken
The shadow cast by age, creeping up
Imprisoning the undying spirit
The lingering longing for the embrace
Of a long lost lover
The never fading memories
Forever tormenting the tortured soul
Oh, unforgiving Almighty
Will there ever be salvation for me?

TIME

The relentless march of time
The cycle reaches the end of the line
The life force ebbing out
With no worthy achievement to tout
Waiting breathlessly for the call
There are no more memories to recall

INEVITABLE EMBRACE

Like a film reel the past rolls on
Each frame a different memory
With different colours and different hues
Some happy, some bring on the blues
Some are bright and bring us smiles
Joyful events and unforgettable moments
Then comes the pain, lots of regret
And an occasional repentance

All treasured and cherished moments
Bringing tears to our eyes
Our vision becomes blurry
And the faces become hazy
As the ebb and flow of life
Course through my weak body
I lie on the bed and wait
For death's inevitable embrace

THE SPARK

A little spark, I know
He gave me when I was born
Though I grew, the spark remained
As tiny as it was
I became worldly and wise, sometimes a little bit crooked
But the spark remained in the innermost crevice
Of my heart, pulsating and flickering. That tiny spark
With its tiny glow, cautioned me when I took a wrong turn
And guided me forward, onto the right path
I know not know what this little spark is
Is it my conscience, the spirit of God or my soul?
Maybe even a hallucination of my logical and rational mind
But I know when I die, I don't want to be
Put in a windowless box, in a tiny hole
Burn me and scatter my ashes far and wide
O'er the oceans and rivers, with the wind so high
That my flaming Spark will get mixed
With all the eternal elements
And be a tiny part of
The ever-expanding universe

DEATH

Time is no man's slave
Impatient as it is to move on
Always patiently waiting in the shadows though
Is the creeping, invisible dark one
To take you beyond the known meadows

SHED A TEAR

Take a shovel and dig me a grave to be put in
Order sixteen red roses to line my coffin
Ride along with the hearse, to my final resting place
Shed a tear but, for my sake, put on a brave face
Carry my memories in your heart and forget them never
But promise me you'll live your life as joyfully as ever

BEAUTIFUL WORLD

Let me soar and touch the clouds and the ends of the sky so high
Let me dive deep into the unknown depths of the oceans
To locate a variety of hidden gems which I would like to possess
Let me catch the sun and wear it as a halo around my head
Let me sail to the crescent moon to gather the shining stars
The fragrance of the grass and flowers on the path already travelled
The innocence of a child, the wisdom of the wise, the love of a mother
Brother and sister, the affection of friends, the blessings of my teachers
The respect of my enemies and the gentle smile of my beloved
Are mine in my beautiful dreamy world, as I lay in sleep unmoved

REBIRTH

Breaking cultural barriers
And the framework of the rational mind
To study the process of unlearning
The prejudices of the learned man
To plunge on like a baby
With gay abandon into
The core existential depths
To emerge with the shroud of awareness
And be reborn once again